Seedling & Sprout
GROWING WITH GOD

PURPLE SPOT SICKNESS

WRITTEN & ILLUSTRATED
BY THE DE VILLIERS FAMILY

WATERBROOK
PRESS

PURPLE SPOT SICKNESS
PUBLISHED BY WATERBROOK PRESS
12265 Oracle Boulevard, Suite 200
Colorado Springs, Colorado 80921
A division of Random House, Inc.

ISBN 1-4000-7196-8

Published in association with the literary agency of Alive Communications, Inc., 7680 Goddard Street, Suite 200, Colorado Springs, CO 80920.

Library of Congress Cataloging-in-Publication Data

Purple spot sickness : a Sprout story / written and
illustrated by the de Villiers Family.
     p. cm. — (Sprout growing with God)
  Summary: When purple spots start popping up all over school, Sprout and
  his friends learn the value of showing others the kindness they would like to
  receive.
  ISBN 1-4000-7196-8
  [1. Sick—Fiction. 2. Schools—Fiction. 3. Conduct of life—Fiction.]
  I. Series.
PZ7.P9779 2006
[E]—dc22
                              2005026531

Printed in China
2006—First Edition

10 9 8 7 6 5 4 3 2 1

"I can see two La-dee-da birds," said Sprout.

"I count three," answered his friend Twig.

"Four, I see four. I win!" Sprout shouted,
looking around.

"I wonder where Petal is this morning?" he said.

They had been waiting for much longer than usual and there was still no sign of her. If she didn't arrive soon, they would be late for school. Mr. Nectar would be worried about them.

Where could she be?

Sprout and Twig waited and waited.
The La-dee-da birds sang again
from high up above.

Twig glanced at his watch. It was almost nine o'clock. "Let's not wait any more," Twig said.

"I think we should wait just a little longer," suggested Sprout.

But Petal still didn't arrive. Just as the two were about to leave, they saw her coming slowly down the path dragging her bag.

"Where have you been?" Twig called.
"Hurry up, it's nearly nine o'clock."

"I'm going as fast as I can," she answered.

Sprout took her hand. "Come on, we're late."
They set off down the path, as fast as
they could, tugging on Petal's hands.

The three friends arrived and everyone had taken their seats already. They slid into their chairs quickly.

Mr. Nectar came
into the room
and asked them
to take out their
reading books.

They worked hard all morning. When it was time for recess, everyone jumped up to go outside and play, except for Petal. She just sat in her seat with her head on the desk.

"Petal, is something wrong?" asked Mr. Nectar. The rest of the class crowded around to see her.

"I feel awful," moaned Petal.

Suddenly—POP!
A bright purple spot appeared
on her hand. Then another one
appeared on her arm, and another
on her cheek.

POP!!

POP!
POP!
POP!

POP POP POP POP POP POP

Before long, Petal was covered with bright purple spots.

"Oh, no," said Mr. Nectar. "You have Purple Spot Sickness. We need to get you home to bed. Don't worry. In a few days the spots will be gone and you will feel much better."

Everyone stared at Petal.

"You look funny, Petal," someone said and everyone giggled.

"She looks like a blueberry muffin," another student said, laughing.

Soon the whole class laughed and pointed at Petal, "Blueberry muffin, blueberry muffin!"

Poor Petal just stood still.
A big tear ran down her cheek.

"Stop right now," said their
teacher. "This is no way to
treat a friend."

Sprout stepped
forward and
took Petal's hand.
"Come on. Let me
take you home."

"I'll help you, too,"
said Twig.

The two friends helped Petal all the way home.
After Petal's mom had settled her into bed,
they brought her a cool drink of dooberry juice.
Then Sprout and Twig fluffed up her pillows,
read her a story, and they all played some
board games.

"You rest now. We'll
be back after school
to see how you're
doing," Sprout said.

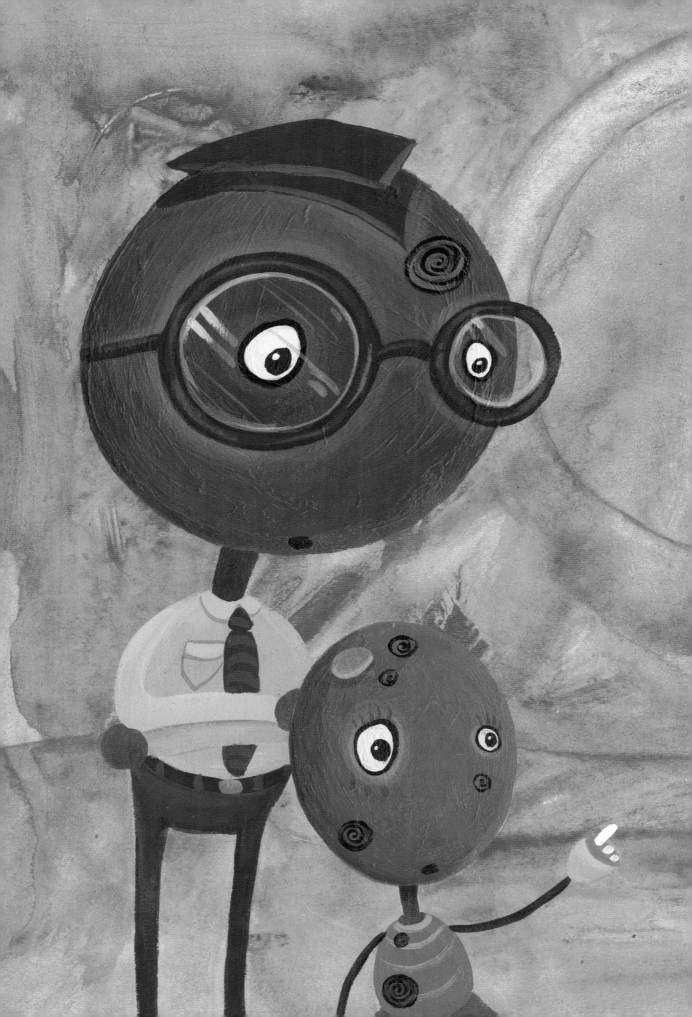

Back at school, purple spots popped up everywhere. One by one, Sprout's friends became sick and covered with spots. Even Mr. Nectar had a big purple spot on his head.

Over the next few days Sprout and Twig were very busy helping their sick friends. They didn't have time for anything else. They fluffed up pillows, poured cool drinks of dooberry juice, made tasty snacks, read stories, and played games until they thought they would drop.

Soon everyone was feeling better
and ready to go back to school,

BUT...

More purple spots appeared!

Only this time the spots were all over Sprout and Twig.

"I feel awful," the two groaned. Their friends crowded around them, but this time no one laughed.

"I know how bad you feel," said Petal. "Now it's my turn to help you feel better."

"I'll help too," another classmate said.

"And so will I," offered someone else."

"And me."
Everyone
wanted to
help them.

So Sprout and Twig were helped to their homes and into their beds. Their friends took care of them. They fluffed up their pillows, read them stories, brought them cool dooberry juice to drink, and made tasty snacks for them to eat until the two friends felt better.

thinklings

1.

How do you think Petal felt when she was being made fun of?

2.

How did Sprout and Twig treat Petal?

3.

Do you always remember to treat others well?

SO IN EVERYTHING, TREAT OTHERS AS YOU WOULD WANT THEM TO TREAT YOU.
MATTHEW 7:12